MW00762954

M.O.D.O.K.

MENTAL ORGANISM DESIGNED ONLY FOR KILLING

LUKE CAGE, HERO FOR HIRE

GREEN GOBLIN

LOKI
MASTER OF MISCHIEF

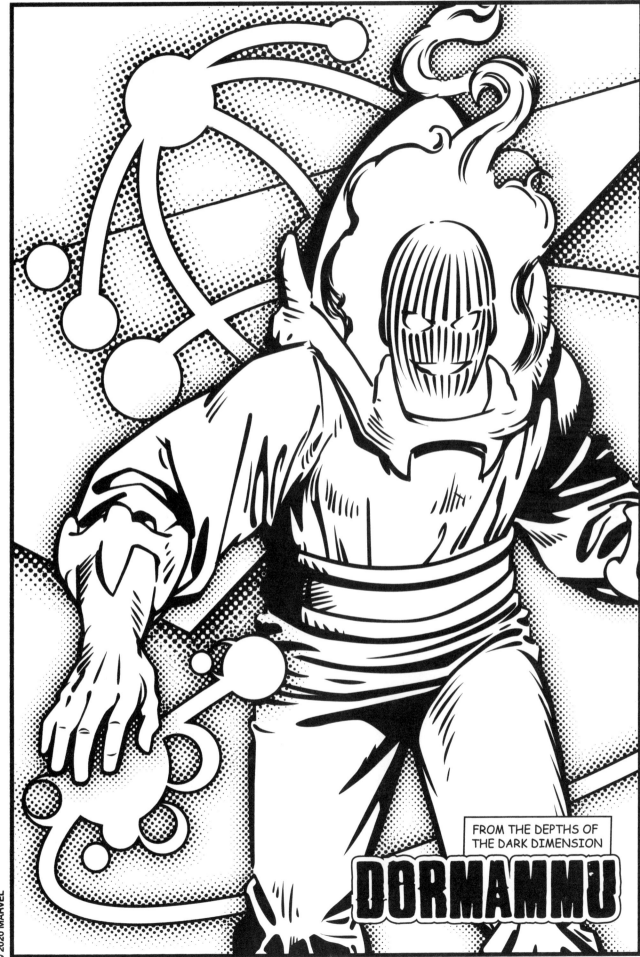

FROM THE DEPTHS OF
THE DARK DIMENSION

DORMAMMU

ANT-MAN

M.O.D.O.K.

MENTAL ORGANISM DESIGNED ONLY FOR KILLING

ARNIM ZOLA

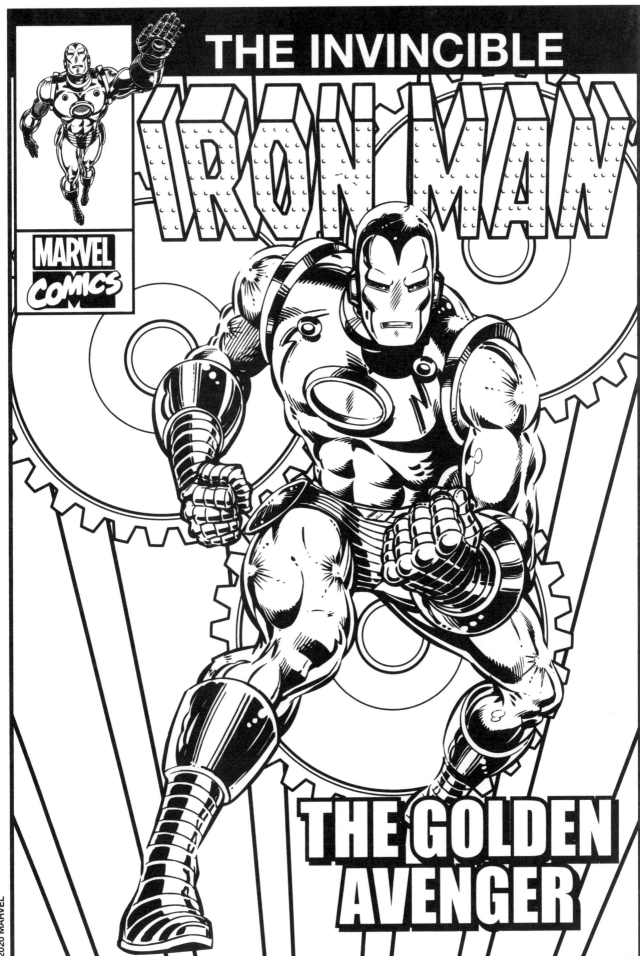

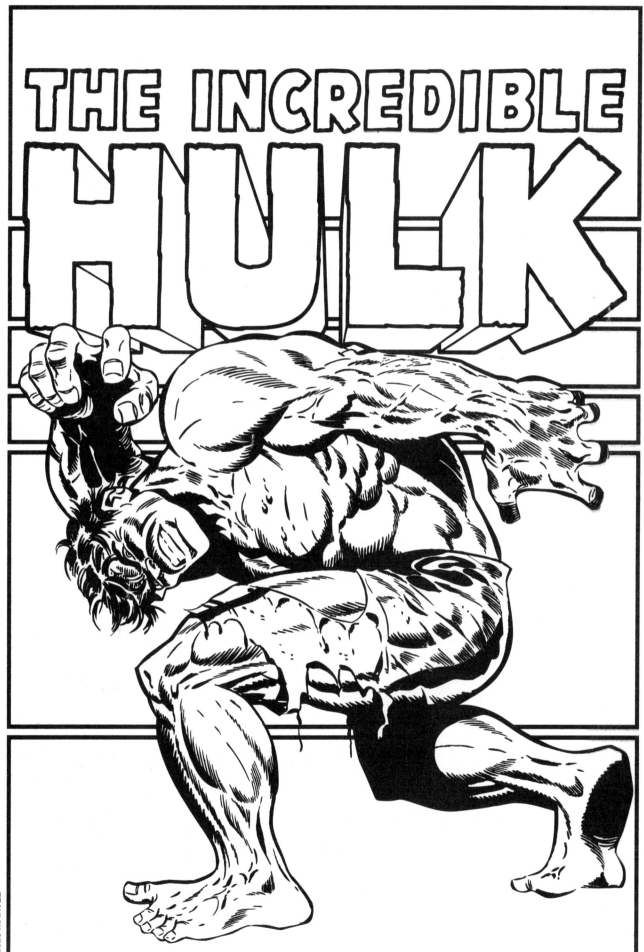

LIVING LEGEND OF WORLD WAR II

CAPTAIN AMERICA

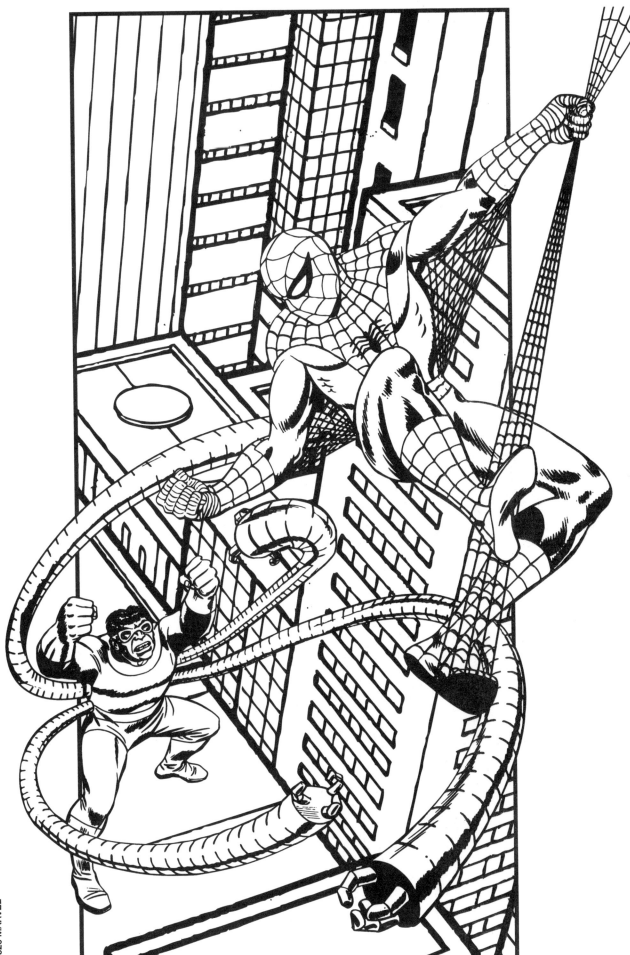

THE INCREDIBLE HULK

MARVEL COMICS GROUP